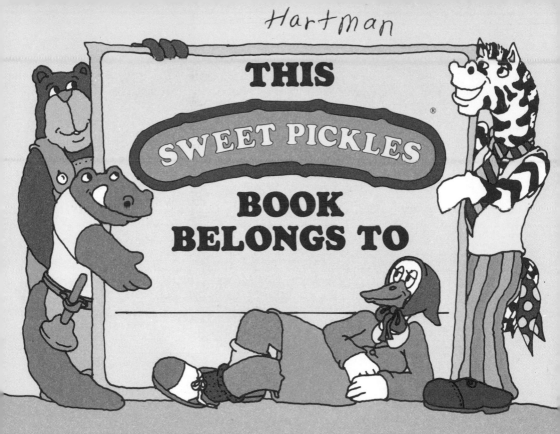

In the Town of Sweet Pickles, the animals get
into and out of pickles because of their all too
human personality traits.

Each of the books in the *Sweet Pickles* series
is about a different pickle.

This book is about robots... and
reading the instructions.

Library of Congress Cataloging in Publication Data

Hefter, Richard.
   Robot S.P.3
   (Sweet Pickles)
   SUMMARY: Clever Camel's Robot creates havoc simply
by following instructions.
   [1. Robots—Fiction]   I. Perle, Ruth Lerner.   II. Title.
PZ7.H3587Ro |E| 81-7759
ISBN 0-937524-09-3   AACR2

Weekly Reader Books Presents

ROBOT S.P.3

Written and Illustrated
by Richard Hefter
Edited by Ruth Lerner Perle

Euphrosyne Incorporated

One morning, in the Town of Sweet Pickles, Clever Camel was unloading strange chunks of machinery from her truck.

Goof-Off Goose, Responsible Rabbit and Enormous Elephant were watching. "What are you doing?" they asked.

"I'm setting up my latest invention," said Camel.
"I call it Robot S.P.3. It does everything!"

"Everything?" cried Rabbit. "What do you mean by that?"

"This robot," said Camel, "will do whatever you program it to do. All *you* have to do is give it careful instructions and it will perform any task!"

Camel finished putting the S.P.3 together. "I have to go back to the shop for some things," she said. "Please watch my robot until I get back. And, whatever you do, don't ask it to do anything until I show you how to work it."

Camel drove off.

Just then, Accusing Alligator came walking down
the street. "What on earth is that pile of junk?" she
said, pointing at S.P.3.

"It's Camel's new invention," said Rabbit. "It's a
robot. It can do anything."

"How does it work?" asked Alligator.
"We don't know," said Elephant. "Camel told us not to do anything with it until she gets back."

"What happens if I push this button?" said Alligator.
"No!" cried Rabbit. "Don't do it!"

Alligator pushed the big button in the robot's chest.
The machine began to whirr and click. Letters
started to flash across the screen in its stomach.
Squeaks and whistles came out of its speakers.
"*I AM ROBOT S.P.3*," it said. "*INSTRUCTIONS,
PLEASE.*"

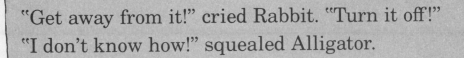

"Get away from it!" cried Rabbit. "Turn it off!"
"I don't know how!" squealed Alligator.
"Give it some instructions," said Goose.

"Robot," yelled Elephant, "bake us some cookies!"
"*HOW MANY?...BEEP...HOW MANY?*" said the
 robot.
"As many as you can!" shouted Alligator.

The robot spun around three times and then whirred and clicked its way into Elephant's house. Everybody followed it.

Elephant tip-toed over to the kitchen door and looked in. The robot was busy tossing cups full of flour into a big bowl. It was humming and whirring and beeping.

Everyone sat down in Elephant's living room and waited for the robot to finish.

"Imagine!" exclaimed Elephant. "All the home-baked cookies we want!" She ran to the kitchen door.

"I can't wait any more," she said. "I've got to taste those cookies!"

Elephant opened the door.

There were cookies everywhere. The table was piled high with cookies. The chairs were covered with stacks of cookies. There were piles and clumps and bunches of cookies all over the counters. The floor was filling up with thousands of cookies!

Then the robot spun around. Letters flashed across its screen. "*NEED MORE SUGAR ... BEEP ... NEED MORE FLOUR,*" it said.

The robot rolled out the back door and clanked across the backyards and into Rabbit's house.

"Oh, my!" cried Rabbit in alarm. "How can we stop it?"

They climbed over the pile of cookies and rushed after the robot.

By the time they arrived, the robot had already produced two thousand fresh baked cookies and was mixing up a new batch of batter. It was humming to itself as it worked. *"AS MANY AS YOU CAN . . . BEEP . . . AS MANY AS YOU CAN!"*

"My milk!" screamed Rabbit wildly. "My flour! My kitchen! STOP! STOP THIS! STOP IT RIGHT NOW!"

"*INSTRUCTION NOT CLEAR*," beeped the robot. "*PLEASE REPEAT*."

"STOP IT!" shouted Rabbit. "HOLD IT! HOLD
EVERYTHING!"

"*STOPPING*," beeped the robot. And it stopped
baking cookies. "*HOLDING EVERYTHING*," said
the robot. It rolled forward and picked up the bowl.
It picked up the table and chairs.

Then it picked up Alligator and Elephant. It picked up the couch and the lamp and the rug and Goose and Rabbit. It rolled out the front door and picked up the lawn mower and Rabbit's car. It rolled down the street, picking up everything.

"*HOLDING EVERYTHING...BEEP...HOLDING EVERYTHING,*" said the robot.

Just then, Camel came walking around the corner.
"Help me!" cried Rabbit. "Stop this thing!"
"You'd better get me out of here!" screamed Alligator.
"Or else!"
"S.P.3," said Camel, "RELEASE RABBIT!"
Rabbit came tumbling out of the pile.

"S.P.3," said Camel, "RELEASE ALLIGATOR AND ELEPHANT."

Alligator thumped to the ground. Elephant followed.

"S.P.3," said Camel, "PUT EVERYTHING BACK!"

The robot turned around and rolled back along the street.

"This is all your fault!" yelled Alligator. "That thing is a menace!"

Camel pulled a small book out of her pocket and stuck it under Alligator's nose. "I told you not to try to use the robot without reading the instructions," she said. "This robot is a very useful piece of machinery, if you learn how to program it the right way with careful instructions."

"I still say it's a menace!" scowled Alligator.

"Wait a minute," cried Rabbit. "Where's Goose?"

"OH, MY GOSH!" screeched Alligator. "That thing still has Goose. Come on! Hurry! We have to rescue Goose!"

They ran to Rabbit's house.

There was Goose, lying on the couch with her eyes half closed, her arms full of cookies.

The robot was stretched out in the chair next to her.

"How did you stop it?" cried Rabbit.

"How did you get it to let you go?" yelled Alligator.

"Well," said Goose. "I looked the robot straight in the eye and said the first thing that came into my mind."

"What was that?" asked Camel.

"I said, 'ROBOT, TAKE A NAP!', " smiled Goose. "And it did!"

Everybody laughed. Except for Robot S.P.3, who was snoring quietly.